Dedicated to all the children who feel they do not fit in.
May you find your direction and a friend to have adventures with.

the polar bear
who hated the cold

THOMAS

AUTHOR
ALISHA HARLAND

ILLUSTRATOR
CAROLINE STORER

There once was a polar bear who **HATED** the cold. His name was Thomas and he lived with his large family on an iceberg in the most icy weather!

Thomas tried so hard to fit in with the other polar bears in their icy games but he was **SOOOOOO** cold!

Thomas wore a scarf, gloves, and a hat
to help keep him cozy.

His gloves kept him warm, but they didn't fit his paws. They made him **slip and slide**.

He tried to warm up and start a fire but
fell right through the ice!

splash!

The other polar bears **LOVED** the cold,
but not poor Thomas.

The time had come for Thomas to start school.

All his classmates played outside the school for their break. Thomas would stay inside to keep **warm and cozy**.

Gulp!

Everyone learned to fish in school.
They would fish with their paws or dive
into the water to catch a fish.
They made a game out of it.

The student with the most fish won the game.
Thomas didn't want to play that game because the
water was **freezing.**

When the school year was over, all the young polar bears would go fishing on their own. It was their way of spending the summer.

They would swim in the icy water and slide down the icebergs! It looked like fun ... but it was **SO** cold!

Wheeeeee!

Thomas didn't want to be cold and he did not want to spend his summer fishing.

Sp.lash!

Finally, the last day of school was here. Thomas found himself on the edge of an iceberg, not wanting to **jump** in with the others.

The others were off racing each other for
the best water to fish in.

Thomas didn't like the cold water so he kept swimming and swimming. The others didn't notice him swimming away because they were too busy fishing.

He swam so far that the water started to become **warm**! He stopped and asked a shark for directions.

The shark said, "Go **THAT** way."

Thomas swam and swam.
He asked directions from a sea turtle.
"Do you know where the warmest water is?"
The turtle said, "Go **THIS** way."

He swam **SO** far
that he bumped
right into an island.

Bump!

Thomas found the island was big, and he wanted to explore. He soon found himself wandering down a big beach. The sand felt **SO WARM** on his paws.

Along the beach, Thomas found an odd looking igloo.
Outside of it, Thomas met Gio.

Gio didn't look like other polar bears.
In fact, Gio didn't look like a polar bear at all.

Thomas asked Gio, "why do you not have fur?"

"**Silly**! I'm a human and humans
have skin and not fur!"

22

"Gio, your igloo looks funny!"
Thomas said with a funny look on his face.

"Oh, Thomas! It's called a house, not
an igloo!" They both **laughed and
laughed.** Soon they became
the best of friends.

23

Thomas and Gio
spent the summer
laughing and playing.

Gio taught Thomas how
to lie in the hammock.

Thomas found out that
hammocks were **NOT**
made for polar bears!

Flop!

Thomas taught Gio how to
fish the only way he knew
how to...**like a polar bear!**

When the summer was over, they both had to return to school. Their adventure was over. Thomas was sad. He had so much fun playing with Gio. He realised that finding the warmth of friendship was the **BEST** kind of warmth!

"When will I see you again?"

Squeeze!

Gio and Thomas agreed they would
meet next summer for another
BIG adventure.

They said goodbye and Thomas
quickly swam home to tell everyone of his
summer adventures.

Splish!

Splash!

THE END

(until the next adventure...)

Printed in Great Britain
by Amazon

38419674R00018